Date: 6/2/15

J GRA 741.5 TEE
Lynch, Brian
Teenage Mutant Ninja
Turtles. Raphael /

TEENAGE MUTANT NINJA TURTLES

RAPHAEL

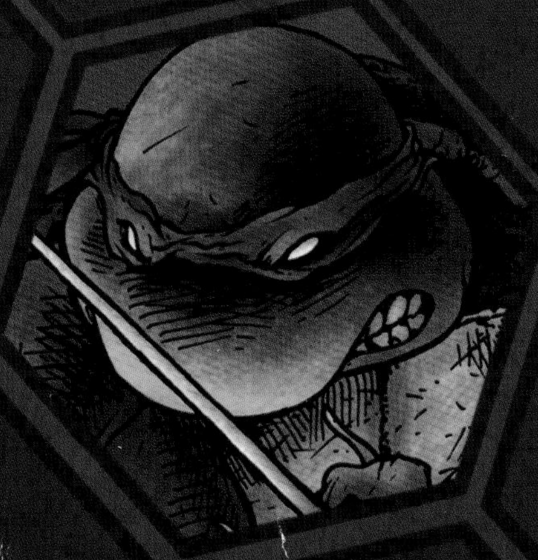

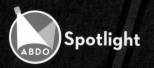

Story by **Brian Lynch**
Artwork by **Franco Urru**
Colors by **Fabio Mantovani**
Lettering by **Chris Mowry**

ABDO Spotlight
IDW

ABDOPUBLISHING.COM

Reinforced library bound edition published in 2015 by Spotlight,
a division of ABDO, PO Box 398166, Minneapolis, Minnesota 55439.
Spotlight produces high-quality reinforced library bound editions for
schools and libraries. Published by agreement with IDW.

Printed in the United States of America, North Mankato, Minnesota.
112014
012015

THIS BOOK CONTAINS
RECYCLED MATERIALS

LIBRARY OF CONGRESS CATALOGING-IN-PUBLICATION DATA

Lynch, Brian (Brian Michael), 1973-
  Raphael / writer, Brian Lynch ; artist, Franco Urru. -- Reinforced library
bound edition.
     pages cm. -- (Teenage Mutant Ninja Turtles)
  Summary: "Raphael is looking for answers and might find them with
Alopex, but can they survive the night?"-- Provided by publisher.
  ISBN 978-1-61479-341-0
1. Graphic novels. I. Urru, Franco, illustrator. II. Teenage Mutant Ninja
Turtles (Television program : 2012-) III. Title.
  PZ7.7.L95Rap 2015
  741.5'973--dc23

                                        2014038233

A Division of ABDO
abdopublishing.com

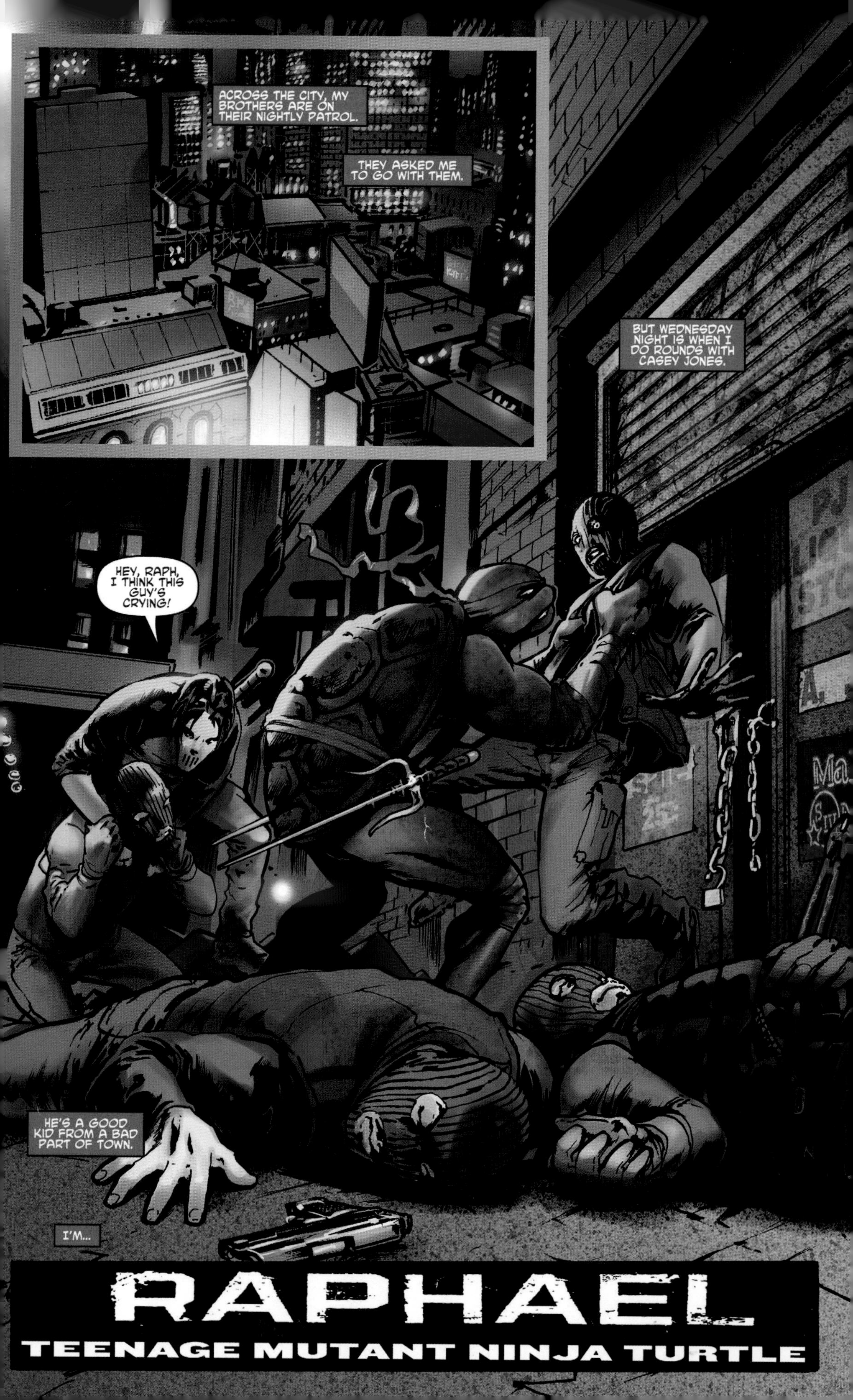
ACROSS THE CITY, MY BROTHERS ARE ON THEIR NIGHTLY PATROL.
THEY ASKED ME TO GO WITH THEM.
BUT WEDNESDAY NIGHT IS WHEN I DO ROUNDS WITH CASEY JONES.
HEY, RAPH, I THINK THIS GUY'S CRYING!
HE'S A GOOD KID FROM A BAD PART OF TOWN.
I'M...
RAPHAEL
TEENAGE MUTANT NINJA TURTLE

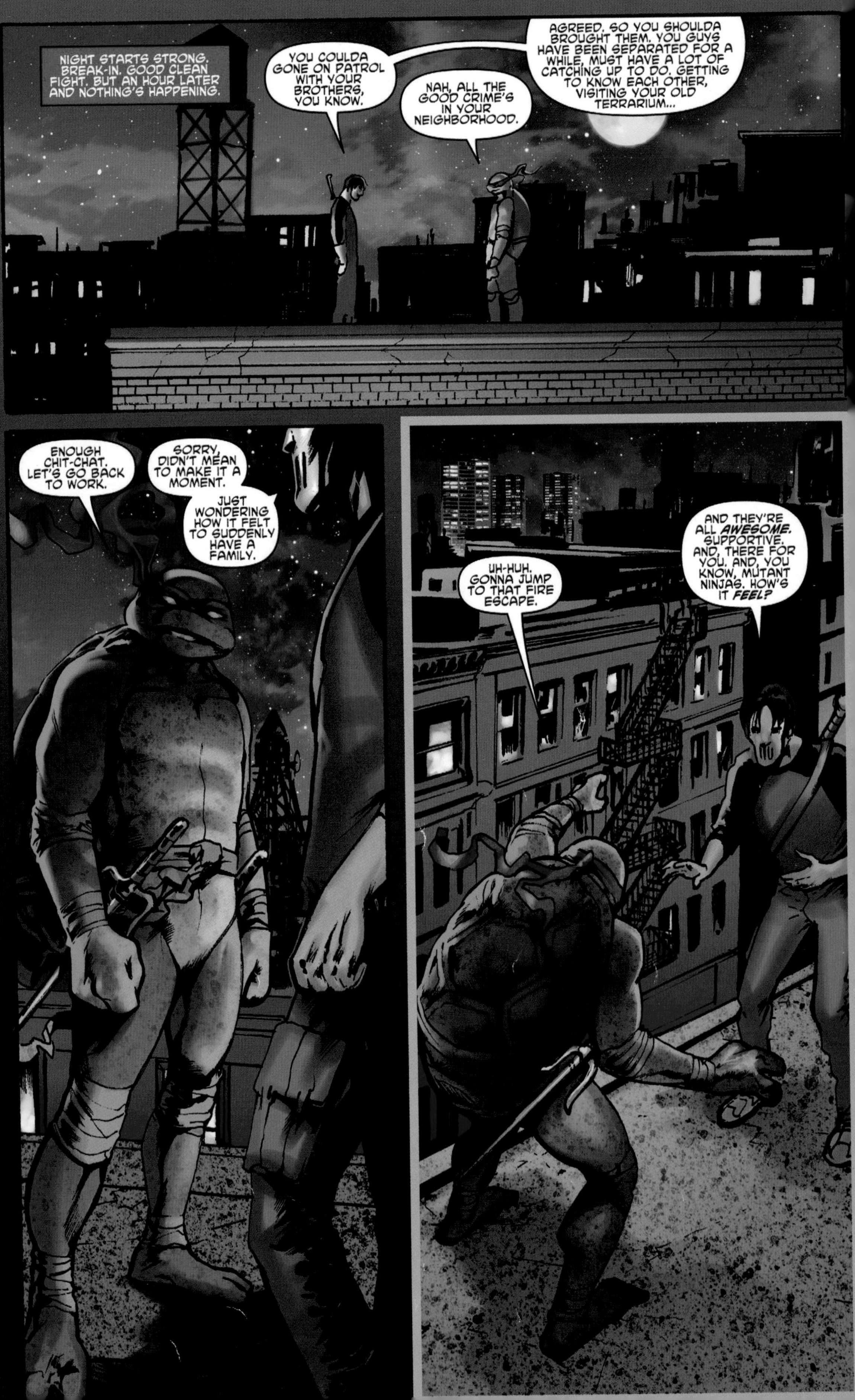
NIGHT STARTS STRONG. BREAK-IN. GOOD CLEAN FIGHT. BUT AN HOUR LATER AND NOTHING'S HAPPENING.
YOU COULDA GONE ON PATROL WITH YOUR BROTHERS, YOU KNOW.
NAH, ALL THE GOOD CRIME'S IN YOUR NEIGHBORHOOD.
AGREED. SO YOU SHOULDA BROUGHT THEM. YOU GUYS HAVE BEEN SEPARATED FOR A WHILE, MUST HAVE A LOT OF CATCHING UP TO DO. GETTING TO KNOW EACH OTHER, VISITING YOUR OLD TERRARIUM...
ENOUGH CHIT-CHAT. LET'S GO BACK TO WORK.
SORRY, DIDN'T MEAN TO MAKE IT A MOMENT.
JUST WONDERING HOW IT FELT TO SUDDENLY HAVE A FAMILY.
UH-HUH. GONNA JUMP TO THAT FIRE ESCAPE.
AND THEY'RE ALL AWESOME. SUPPORTIVE. AND, THERE FOR YOU. AND, YOU KNOW, MUTANT NINJAS. HOW'S IT FEEL?

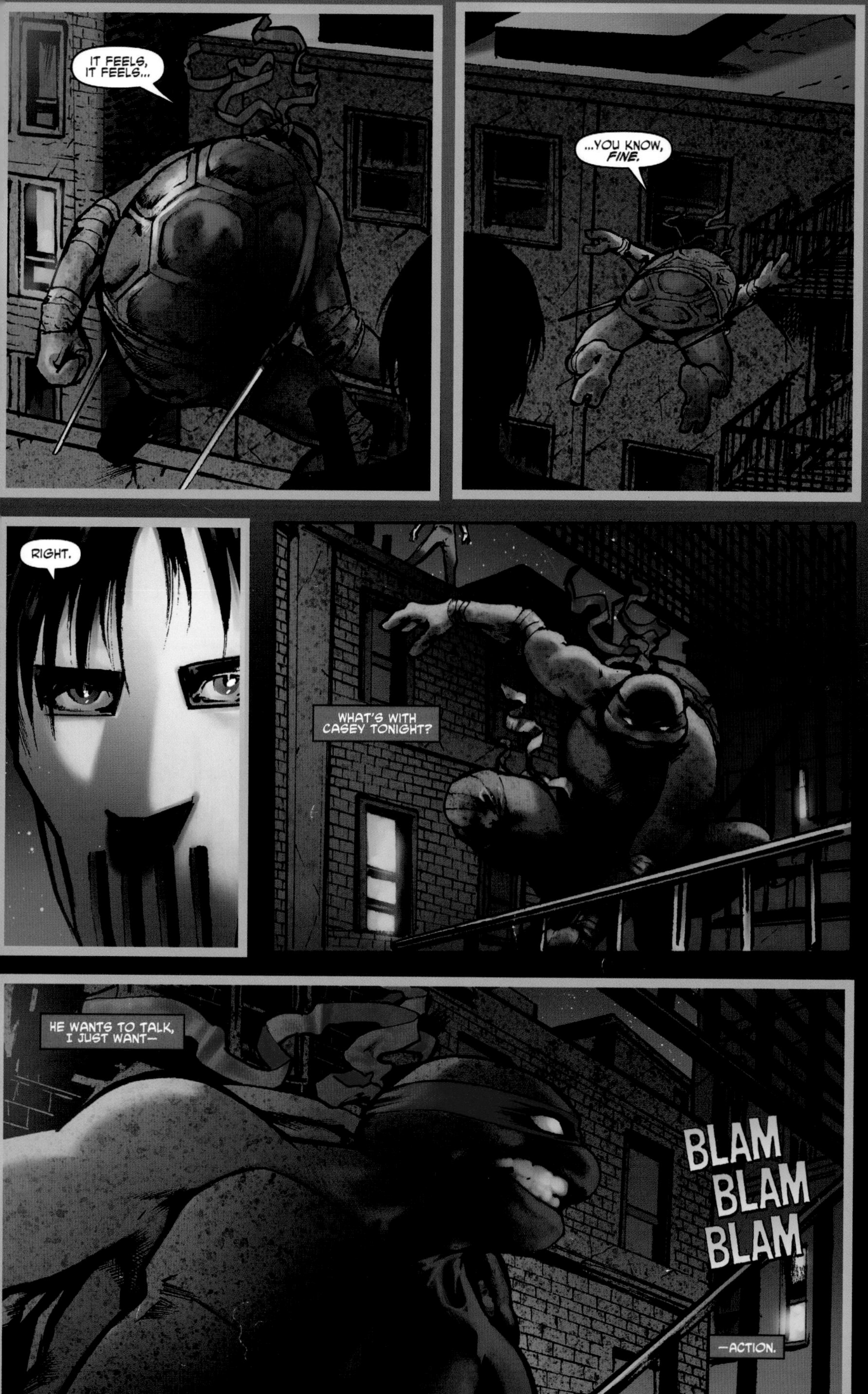
IT FEELS,
IT FEELS...
...YOU KNOW,
FINE.
RIGHT.
WHAT'S WITH
CASEY TONIGHT?
HE WANTS TO TALK,
I JUST WANT—
BLAM
BLAM
BLAM
—ACTION.

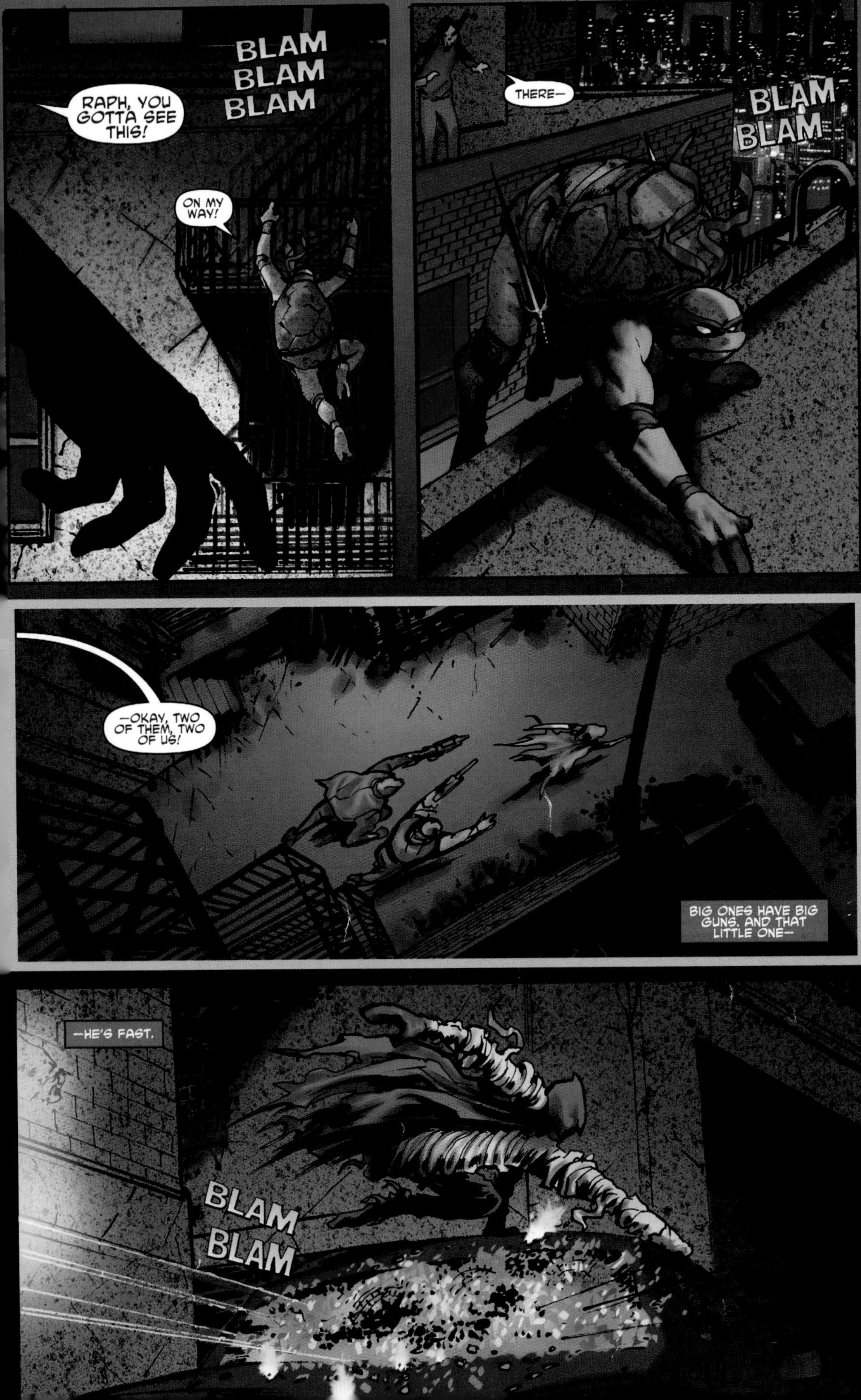
BLAM
BLAM
BLAM
RAPH, YOU GOTTA SEE THIS!
ON MY WAY!
THERE—
BLAM
BLAM
—OKAY, TWO OF THEM, TWO OF US!
BIG ONES HAVE BIG GUNS. AND THAT LITTLE ONE—
—HE'S FAST.
BLAM
BLAM

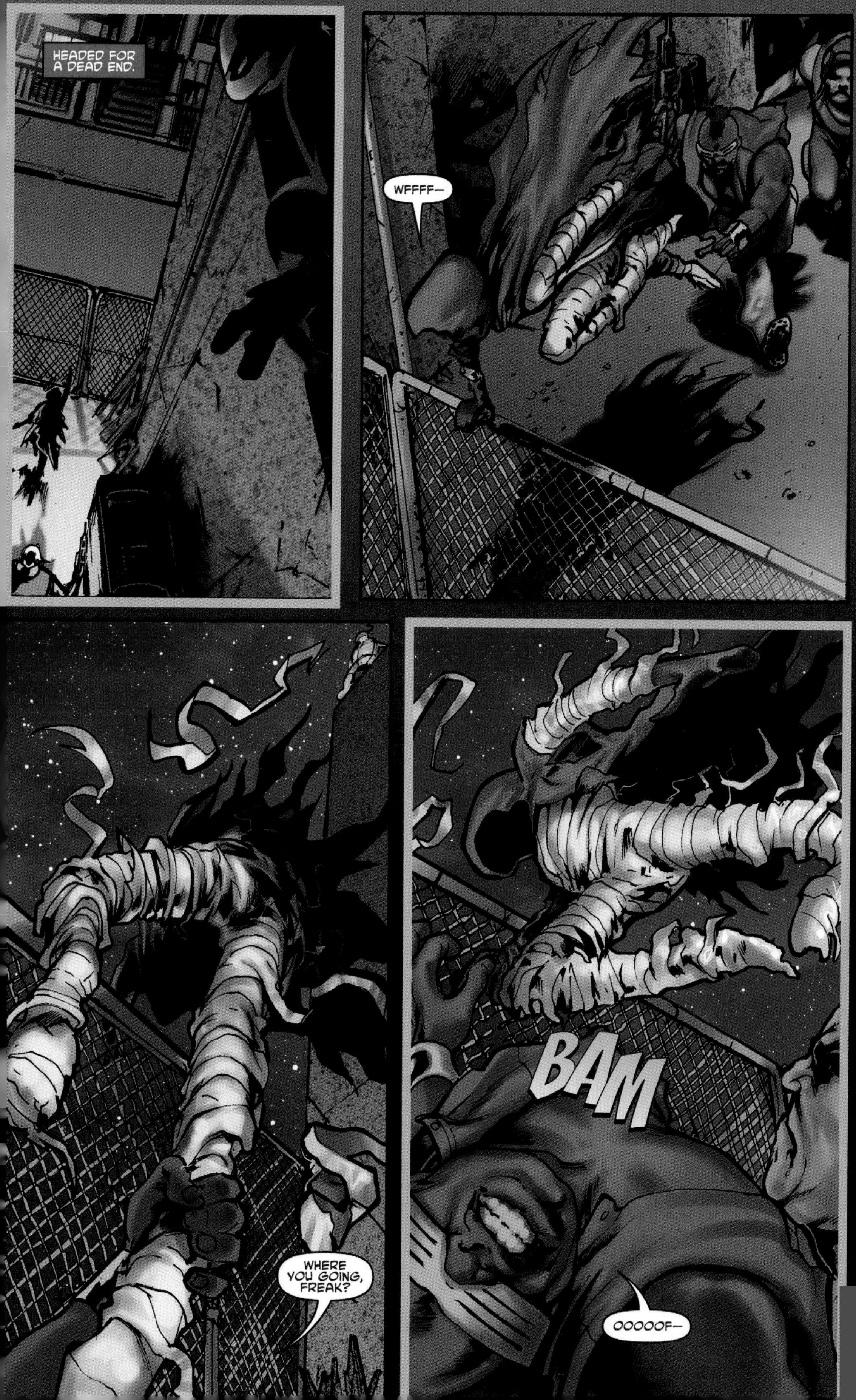
HEADED FOR A DEAD END.
WFFFF—
WHERE YOU GOING, FREAK?
BAM
OOOOOF—

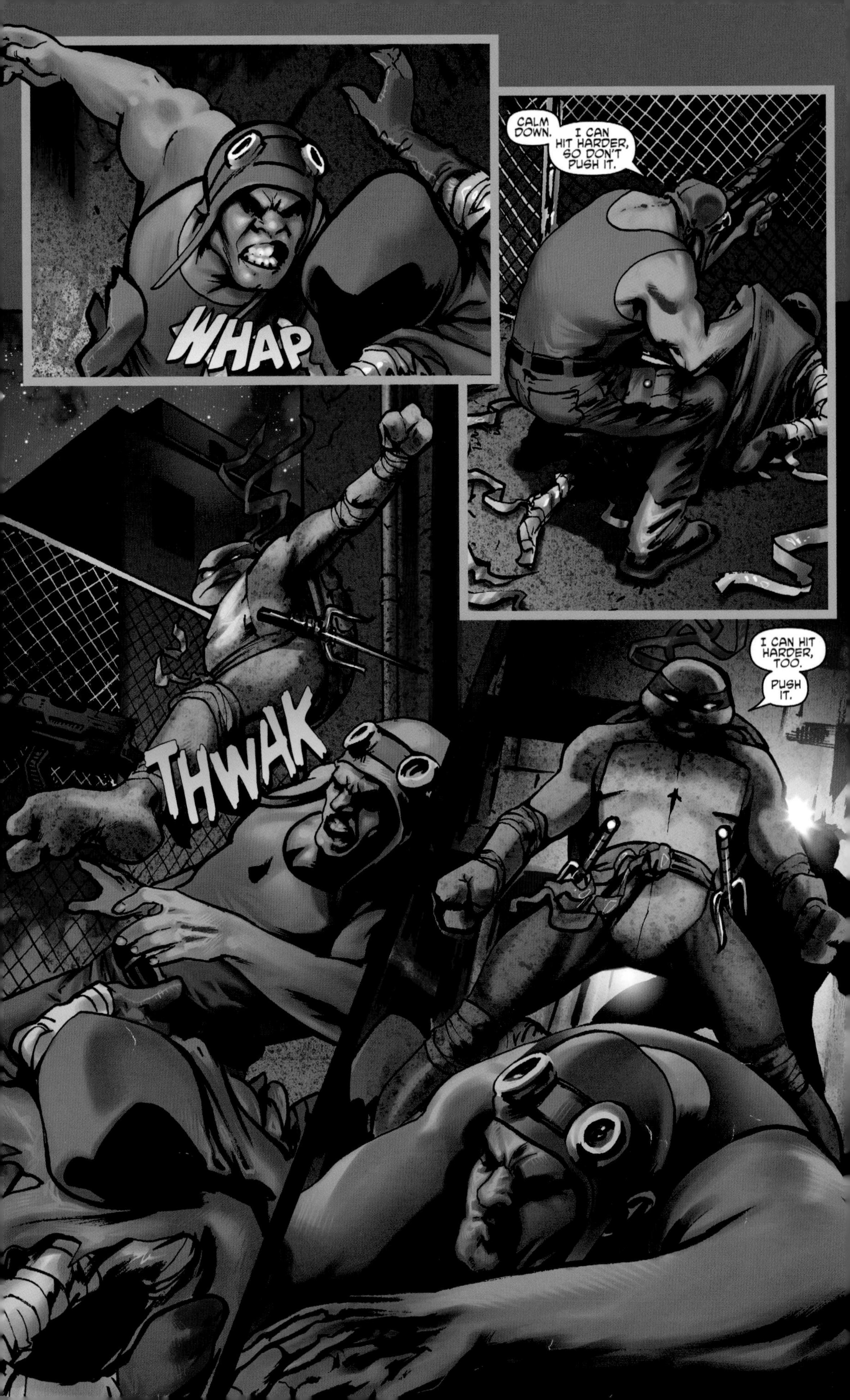
WHAP
CALM DOWN.
I CAN HIT HARDER, SO DON'T PUSH IT.
THWAK
I CAN HIT HARDER, TOO.
PUSH IT.

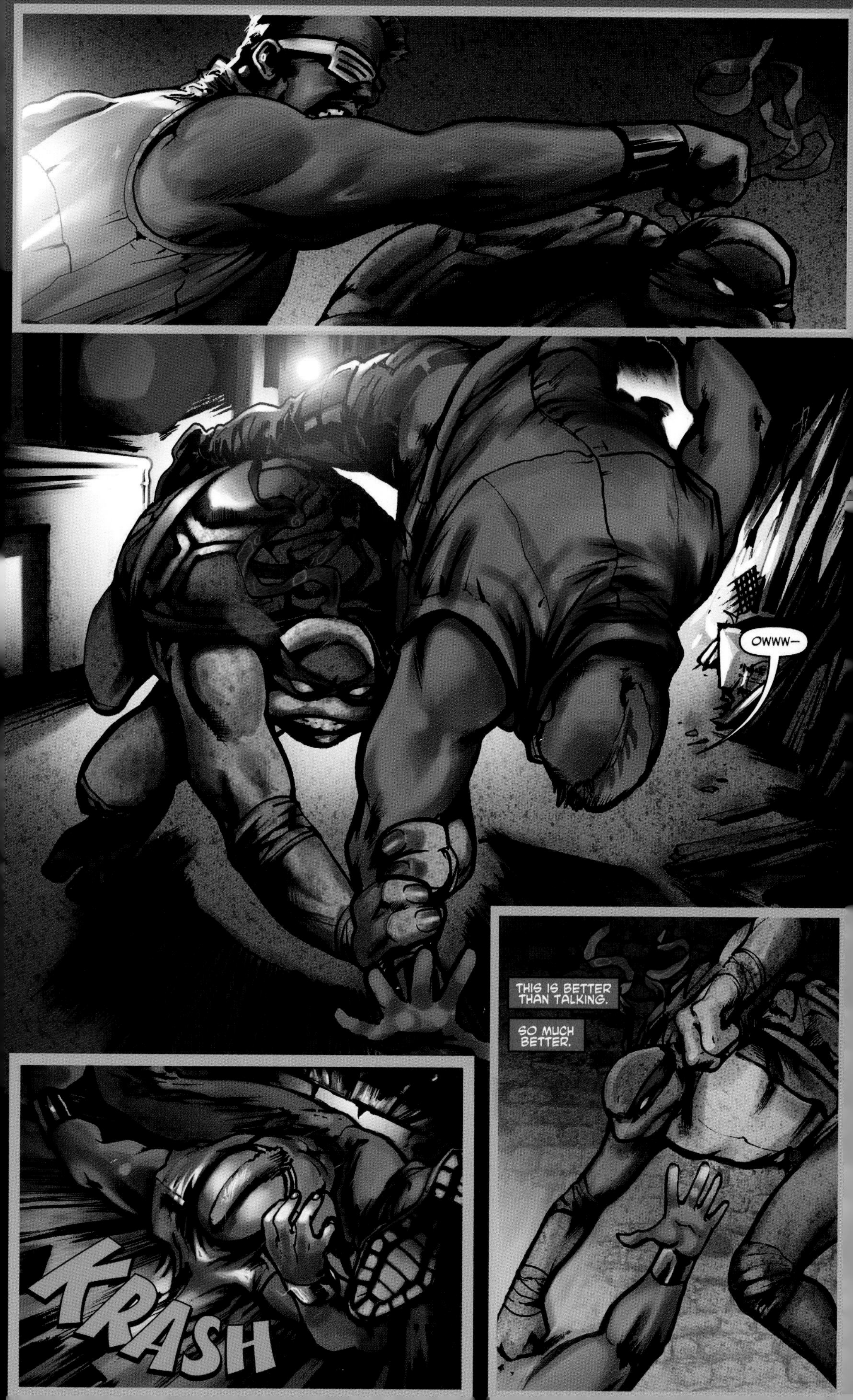
OWWW—
THIS IS BETTER THAN TALKING.
SO MUCH BETTER.
KRASH

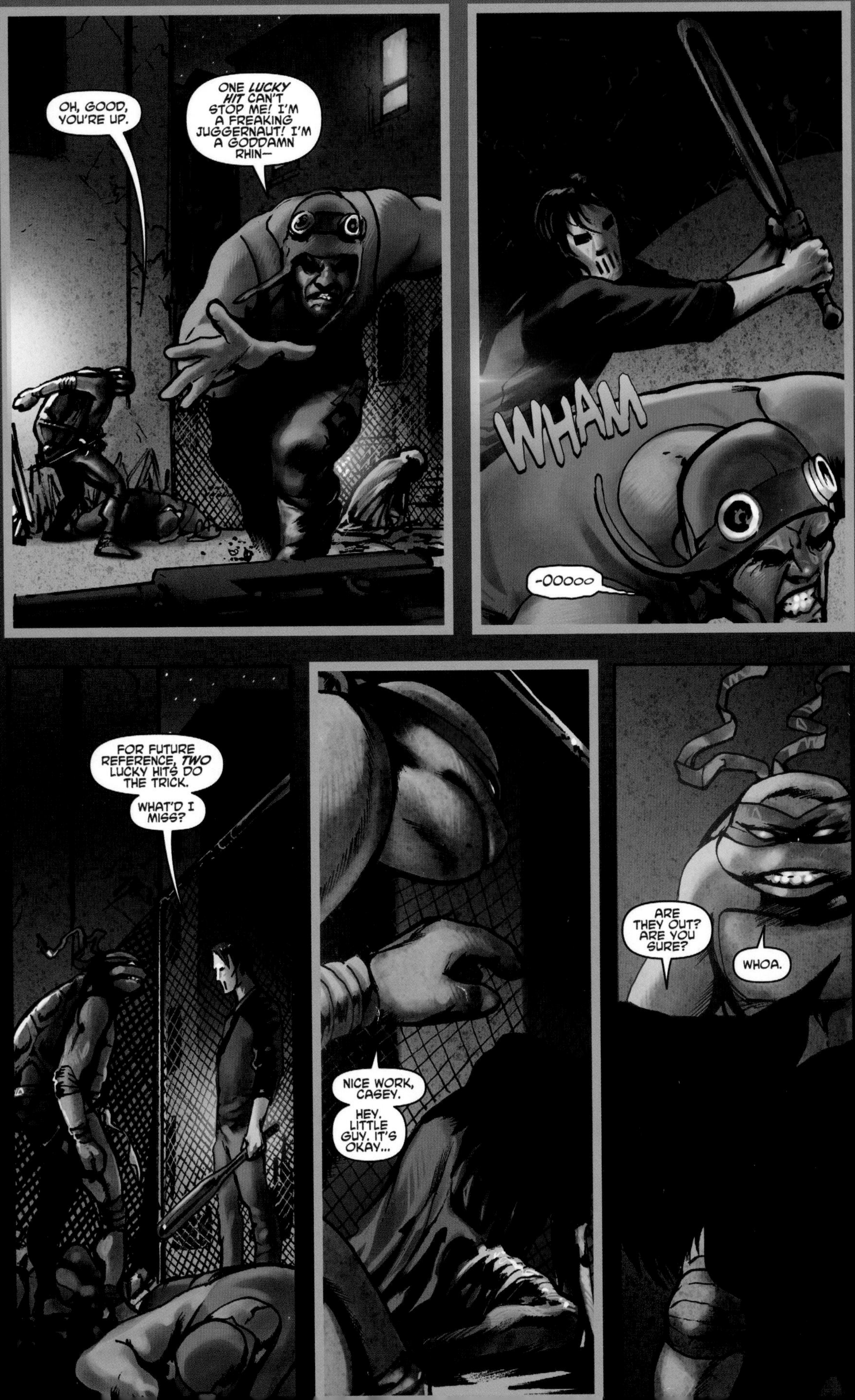
OH, GOOD, YOU'RE UP.
ONE LUCKY HIT CAN'T STOP ME! I'M A FREAKING JUGGERNAUT! I'M A GODDAMN RHIN—
WHAM
-OOOOO
FOR FUTURE REFERENCE, TWO LUCKY HITS DO THE TRICK.
WHAT'D I MISS?
NICE WORK, CASEY.
HEY. LITTLE GUY. IT'S OKAY...
ARE THEY OUT? ARE YOU SURE?
WHOA.

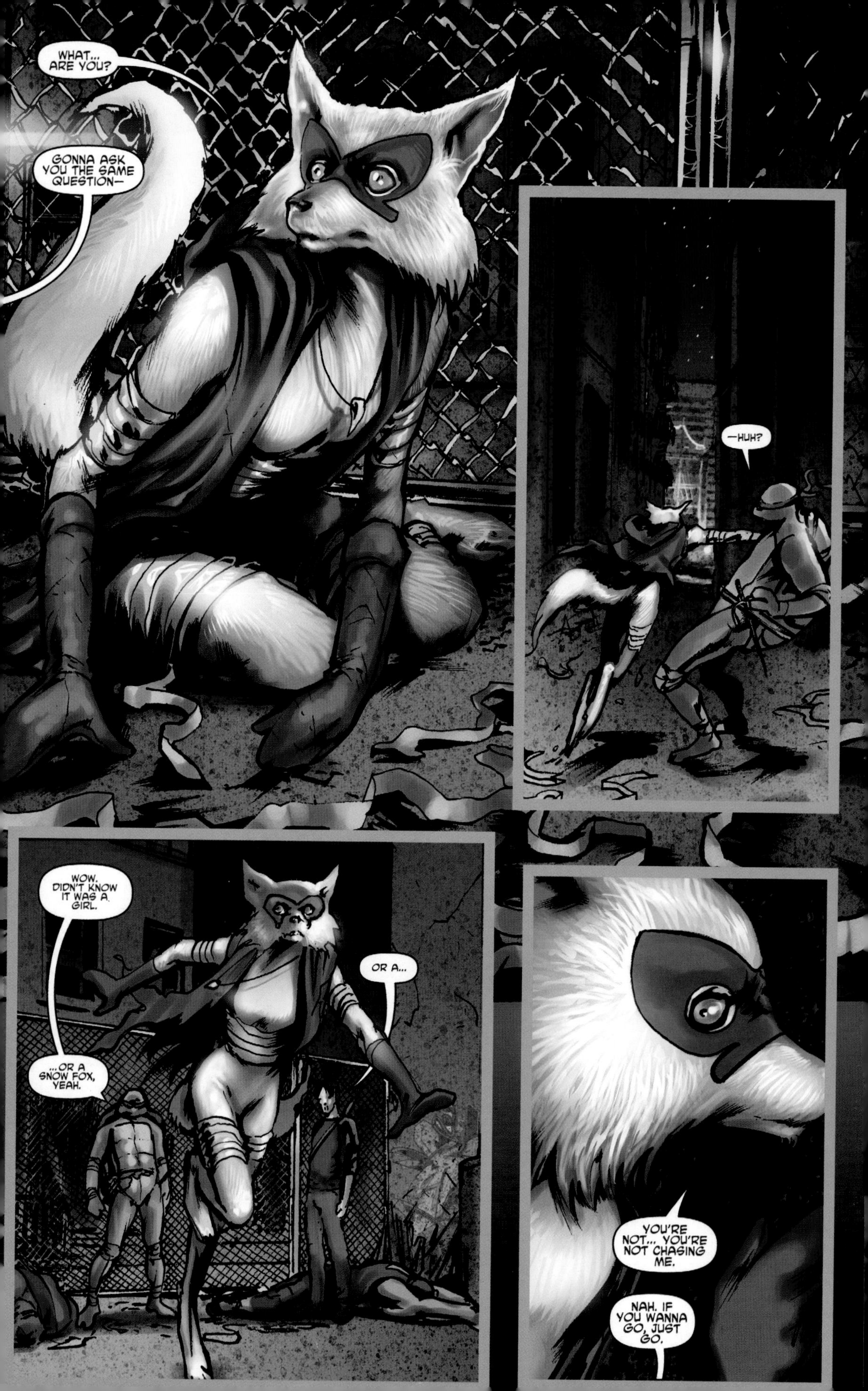
WHAT... ARE YOU?
GONNA ASK YOU THE SAME QUESTION—
—HUH?
WOW. DIDN'T KNOW IT WAS A GIRL.
OR A...
...OR A SNOW FOX, YEAH.
YOU'RE NOT... YOU'RE NOT CHASING ME.
NAH. IF YOU WANNA GO, JUST GO.

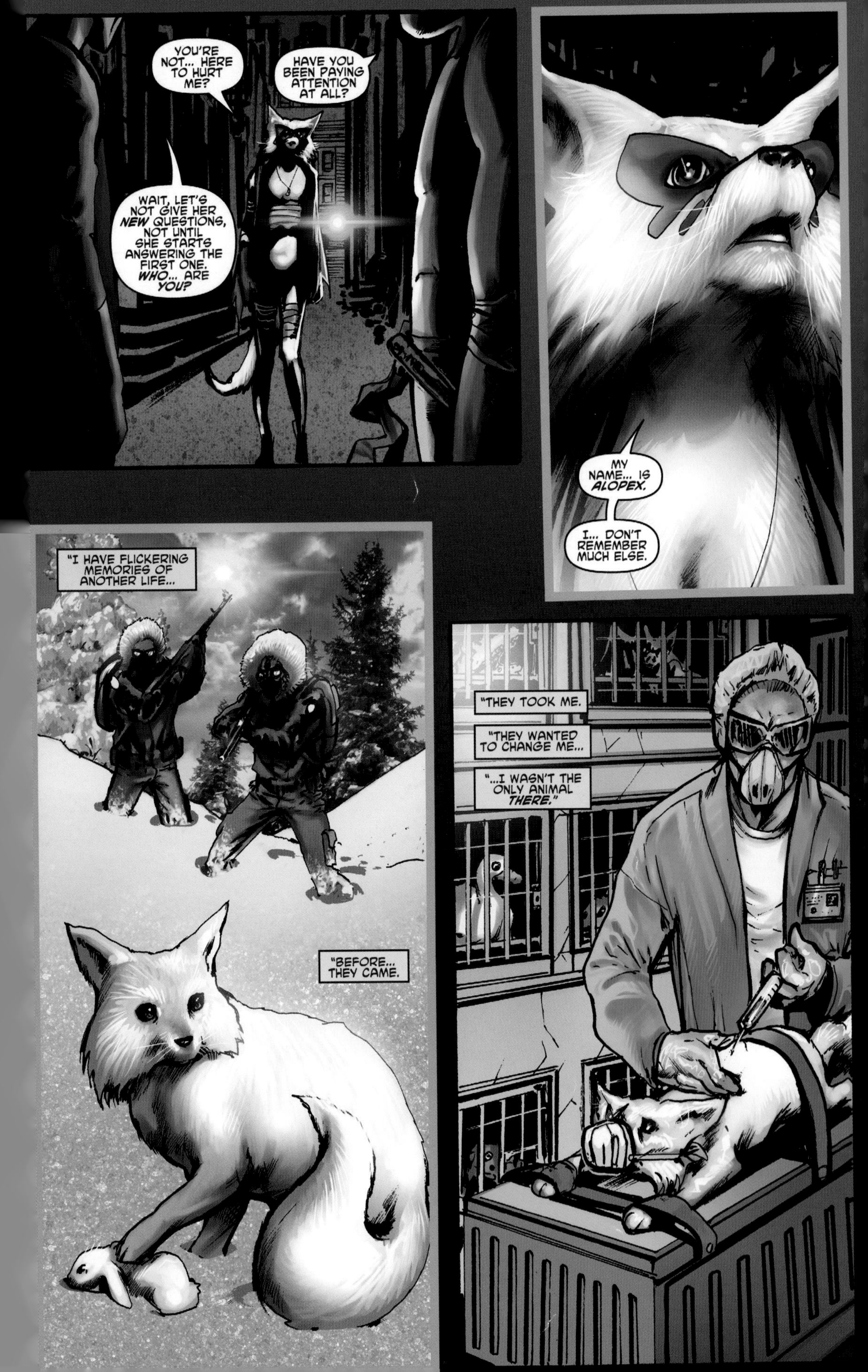
YOU'RE NOT... HERE TO HURT ME?
HAVE YOU BEEN PAYING ATTENTION AT ALL?
WAIT, LET'S NOT GIVE HER *NEW* QUESTIONS, NOT UNTIL SHE STARTS ANSWERING THE FIRST ONE. *WHO*... ARE *YOU*?
MY NAME... IS *ALOPEX.*
I... DON'T REMEMBER MUCH ELSE.
"I HAVE FLICKERING MEMORIES OF ANOTHER LIFE...
"BEFORE... THEY CAME.
"THEY TOOK ME.
"THEY WANTED TO CHANGE ME...
"...I WASN'T THE ONLY ANIMAL *THERE.*"

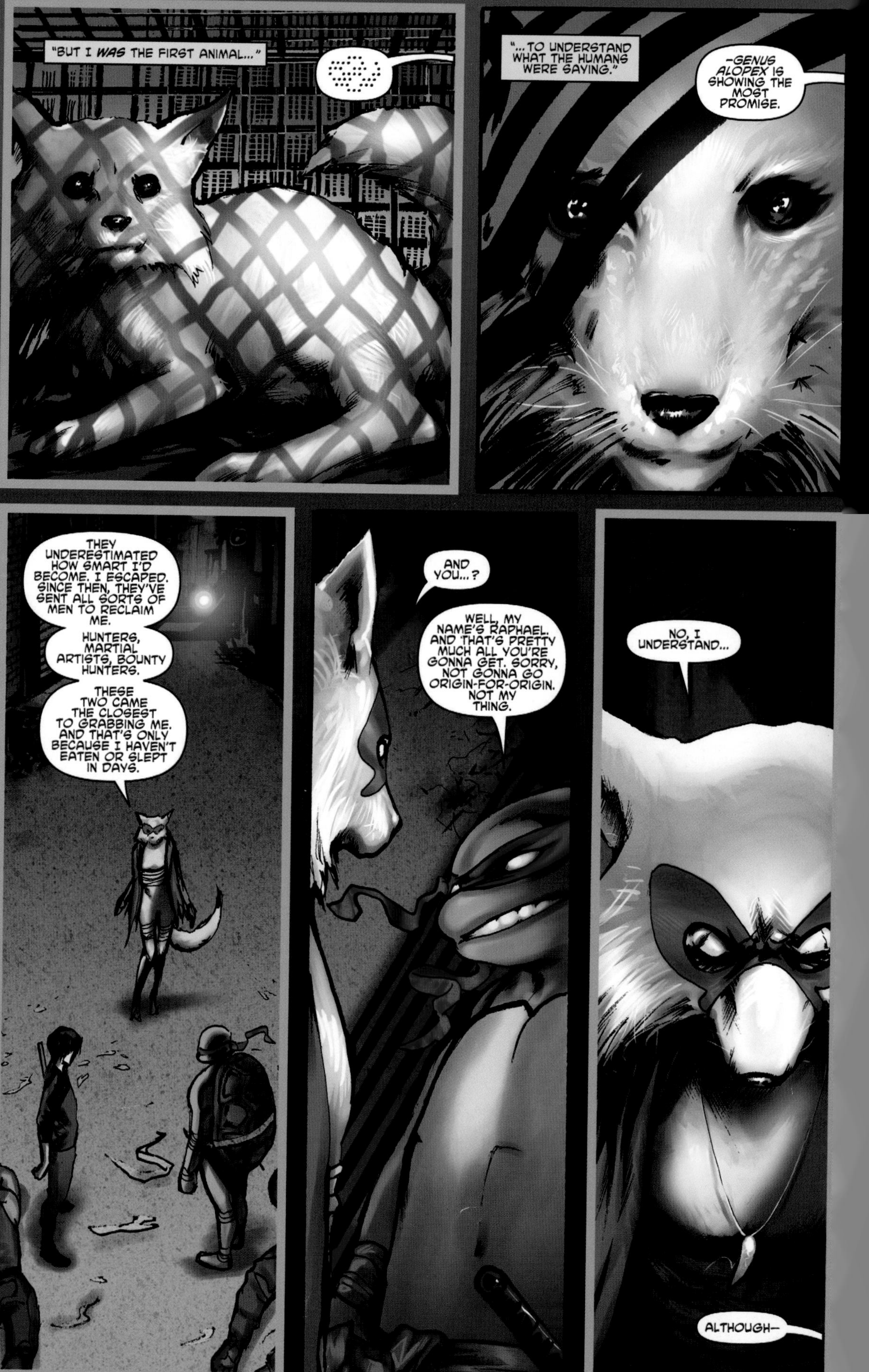
"BUT I WAS THE FIRST ANIMAL..."
"...TO UNDERSTAND WHAT THE HUMANS WERE SAYING."
-GENUS ALOPEX IS SHOWING THE MOST PROMISE.
THEY UNDERESTIMATED HOW SMART I'D BECOME. I ESCAPED. SINCE THEN, THEY'VE SENT ALL SORTS OF MEN TO RECLAIM ME.
HUNTERS, MARTIAL ARTISTS, BOUNTY HUNTERS.
THESE TWO CAME THE CLOSEST TO GRABBING ME. AND THAT'S ONLY BECAUSE I HAVEN'T EATEN OR SLEPT IN DAYS.
AND YOU...?
WELL, MY NAME'S RAPHAEL. AND THAT'S PRETTY MUCH ALL YOU'RE GONNA GET. SORRY, NOT GONNA GO ORIGIN-FOR-ORIGIN. NOT MY THING.
NO, I UNDERSTAND...
ALTHOUGH—

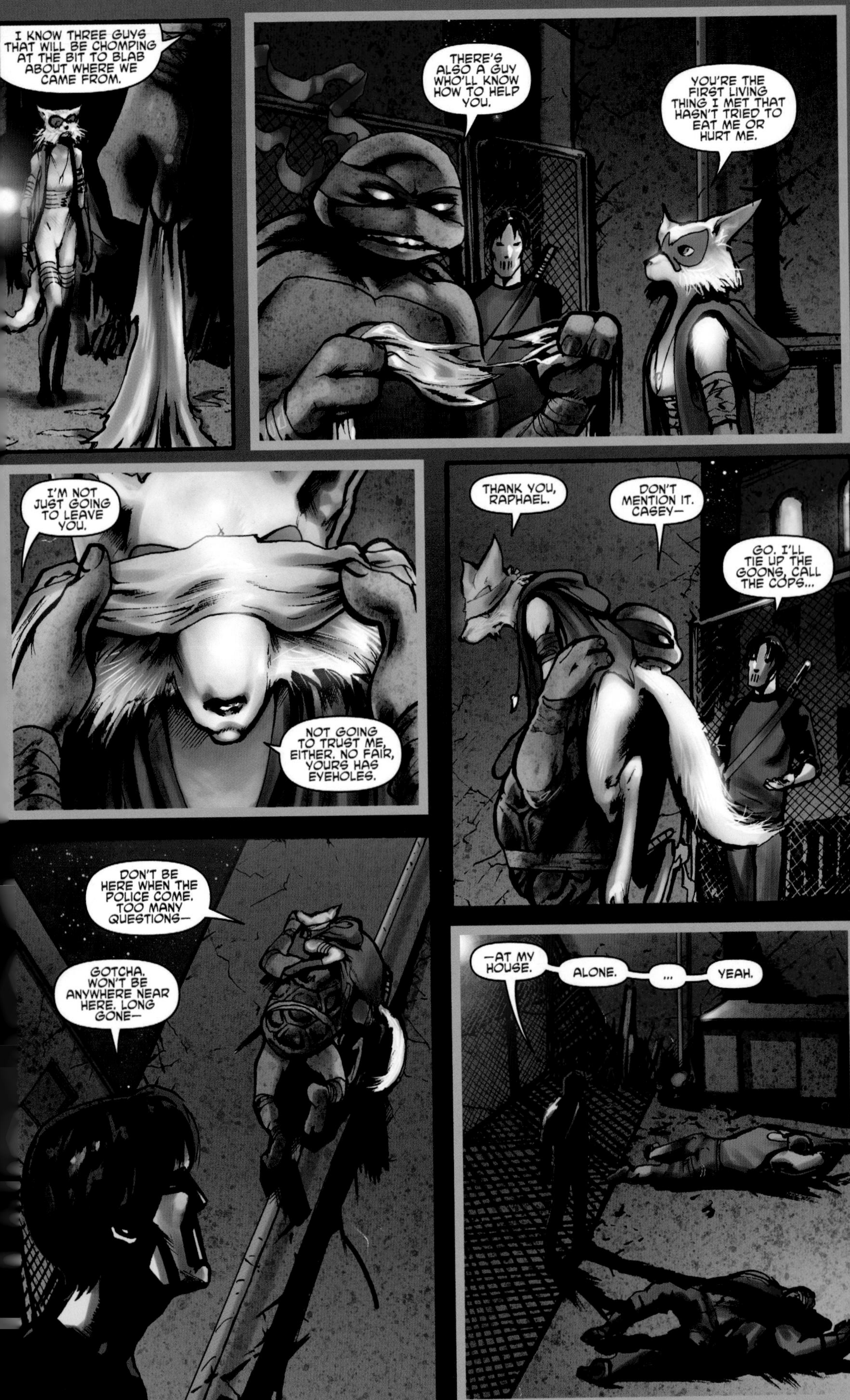
I KNOW THREE GUYS THAT WILL BE CHOMPING AT THE BIT TO BLAB ABOUT WHERE WE CAME FROM.
THERE'S ALSO A GUY WHO'LL KNOW HOW TO HELP YOU.
YOU'RE THE FIRST LIVING THING I MET THAT HASN'T TRIED TO EAT ME OR HURT ME.
I'M NOT JUST GOING TO LEAVE YOU.
NOT GOING TO TRUST ME, EITHER. NO FAIR, YOURS HAS EYEHOLES.
THANK YOU, RAPHAEL.
DON'T MENTION IT. CASEY—
GO. I'LL TIE UP THE GOONS, CALL THE COPS...
DON'T BE HERE WHEN THE POLICE COME. TOO MANY QUESTIONS—
GOTCHA. WON'T BE ANYWHERE NEAR HERE. LONG GONE—
—AT MY HOUSE.
ALONE.
...
YEAH.

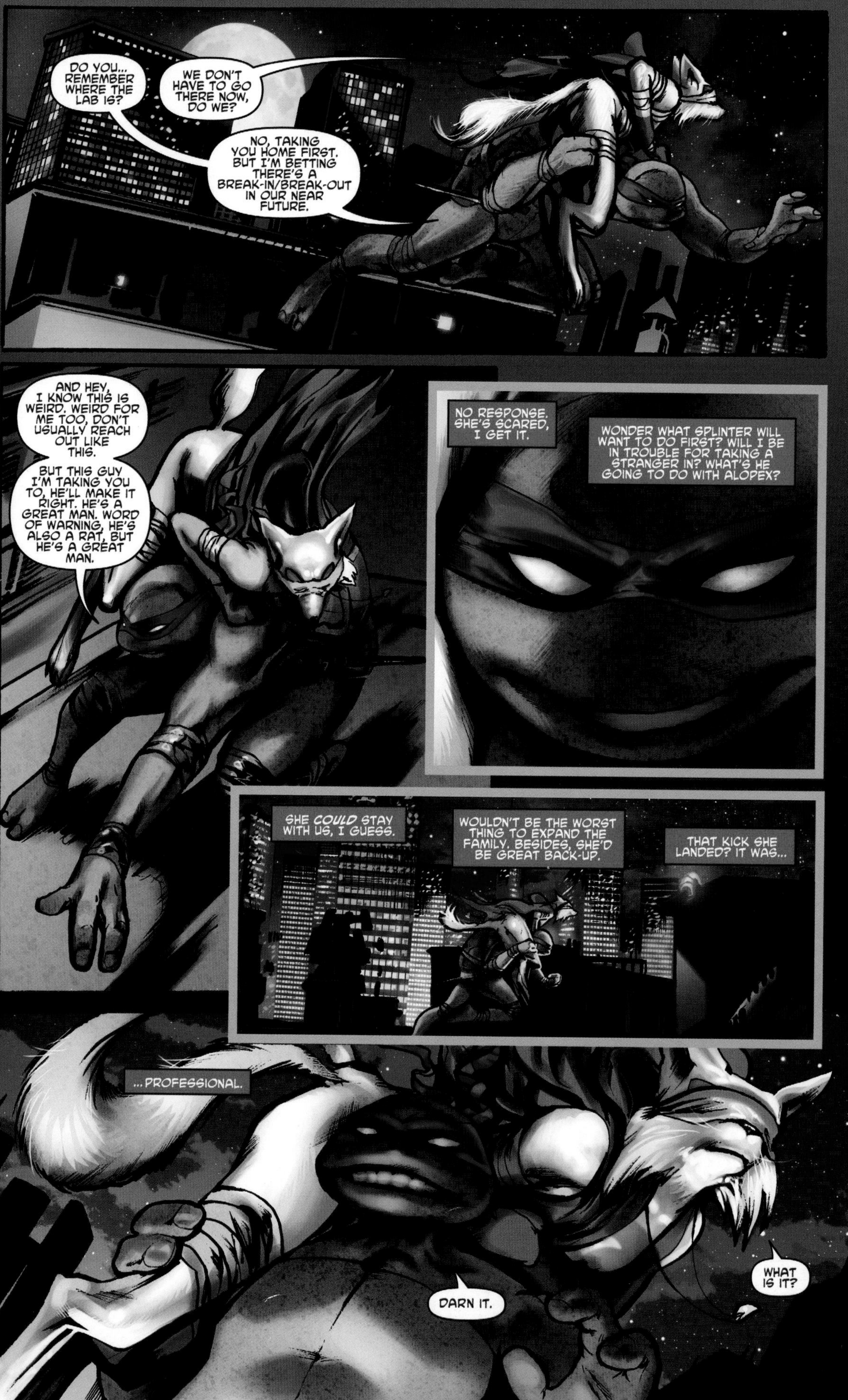
DO YOU... REMEMBER WHERE THE LAB IS?
WE DON'T HAVE TO GO THERE NOW, DO WE?
NO, TAKING YOU HOME FIRST. BUT I'M BETTING THERE'S A BREAK-IN/BREAK-OUT IN OUR NEAR FUTURE.
AND HEY, I KNOW THIS IS WEIRD. WEIRD FOR ME TOO, DON'T USUALLY REACH OUT LIKE THIS.
BUT THIS GUY I'M TAKING YOU TO, HE'LL MAKE IT RIGHT. HE'S A GREAT MAN. WORD OF WARNING, HE'S ALSO A RAT, BUT HE'S A GREAT MAN.
NO RESPONSE. SHE'S SCARED, I GET IT.
WONDER WHAT SPLINTER WILL WANT TO DO FIRST? WILL I BE IN TROUBLE FOR TAKING A STRANGER IN? WHAT'S HE GOING TO DO WITH ALOPEX?
SHE *COULD* STAY WITH US, I GUESS.
WOULDN'T BE THE WORST THING TO EXPAND THE FAMILY. BESIDES, SHE'D BE GREAT BACK-UP.
THAT KICK SHE LANDED? IT WAS...
...PROFESSIONAL.
DARN IT.
WHAT IS IT?

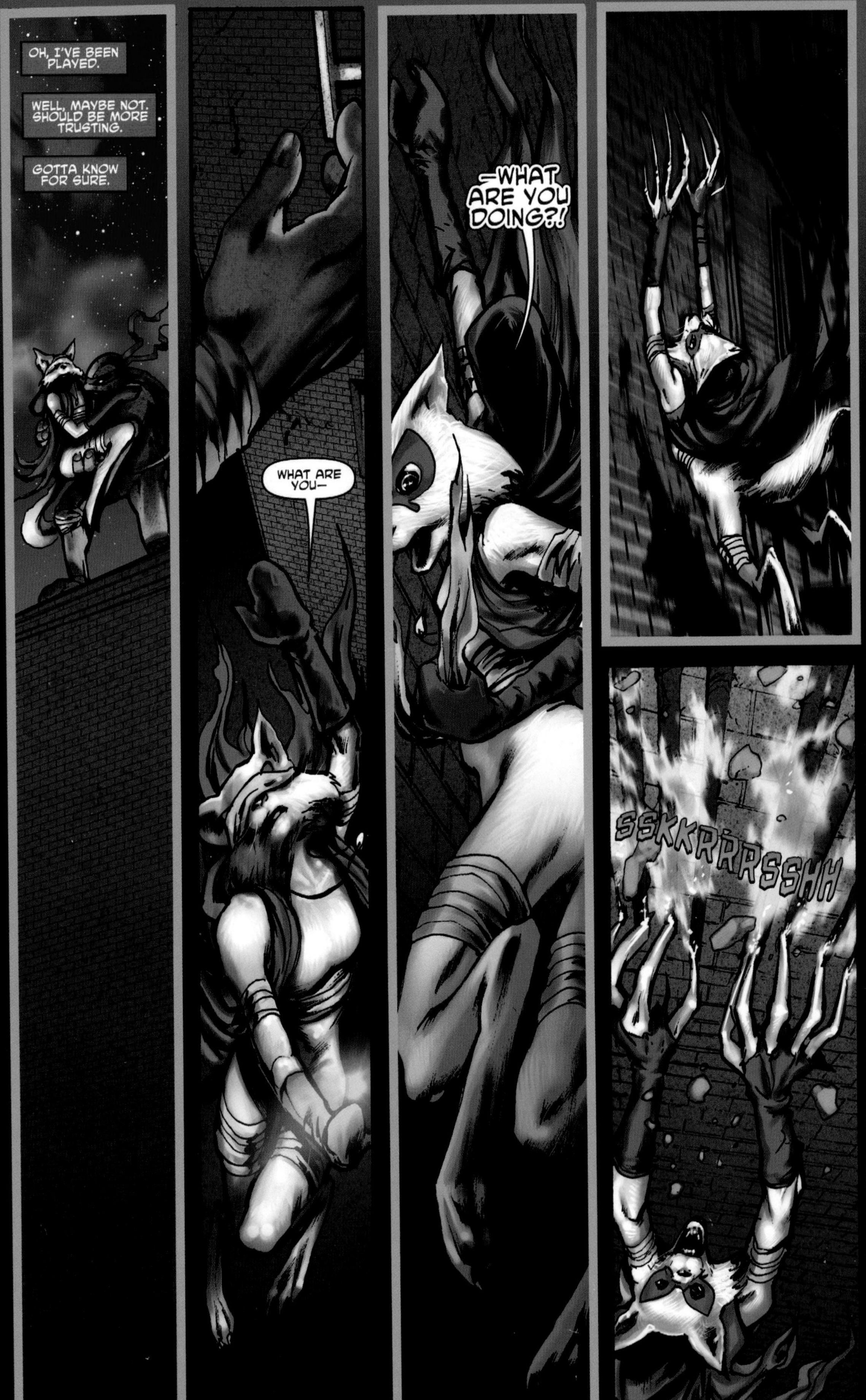
OH, I'VE BEEN PLAYED.
WELL, MAYBE NOT. SHOULD BE MORE TRUSTING.
GOTTA KNOW FOR SURE.
WHAT ARE YOU—
—WHAT ARE YOU DOING?!
SSKKRRRRSSHH

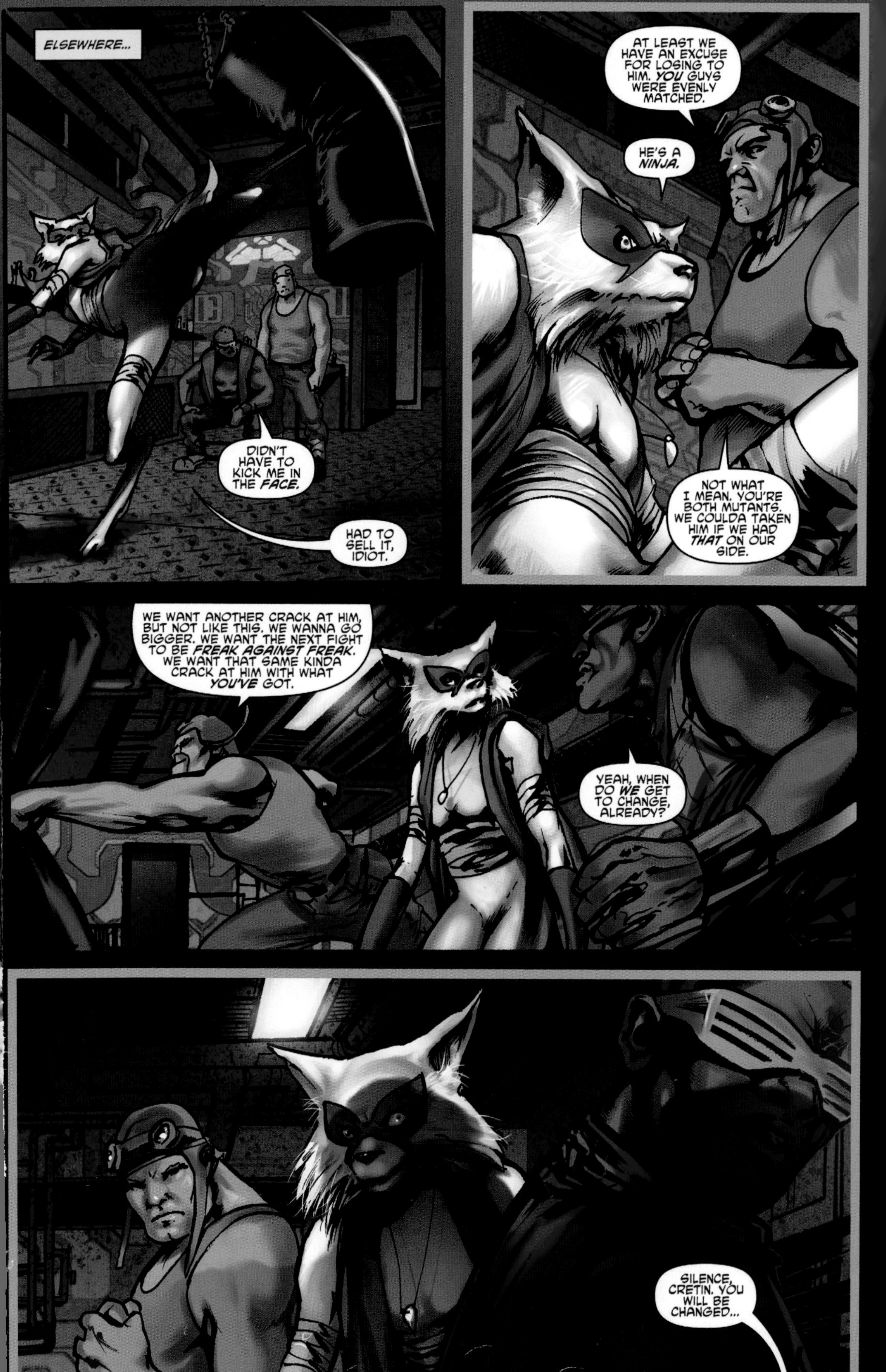
ELSEWHERE...
DIDN'T HAVE TO KICK ME IN THE FACE.
HAD TO SELL IT, IDIOT.
AT LEAST WE HAVE AN EXCUSE FOR LOSING TO HIM. YOU GUYS WERE EVENLY MATCHED.
HE'S A NINJA.
NOT WHAT I MEAN. YOU'RE BOTH MUTANTS. WE COULDA TAKEN HIM IF WE HAD THAT ON OUR SIDE.
WE WANT ANOTHER CRACK AT HIM, BUT NOT LIKE THIS. WE WANNA GO BIGGER. WE WANT THE NEXT FIGHT TO BE FREAK AGAINST FREAK. WE WANT THAT SAME KINDA CRACK AT HIM WITH WHAT YOU'VE GOT.
YEAH, WHEN DO WE GET TO CHANGE, ALREADY?
SILENCE, CRETIN. YOU WILL BE CHANGED...

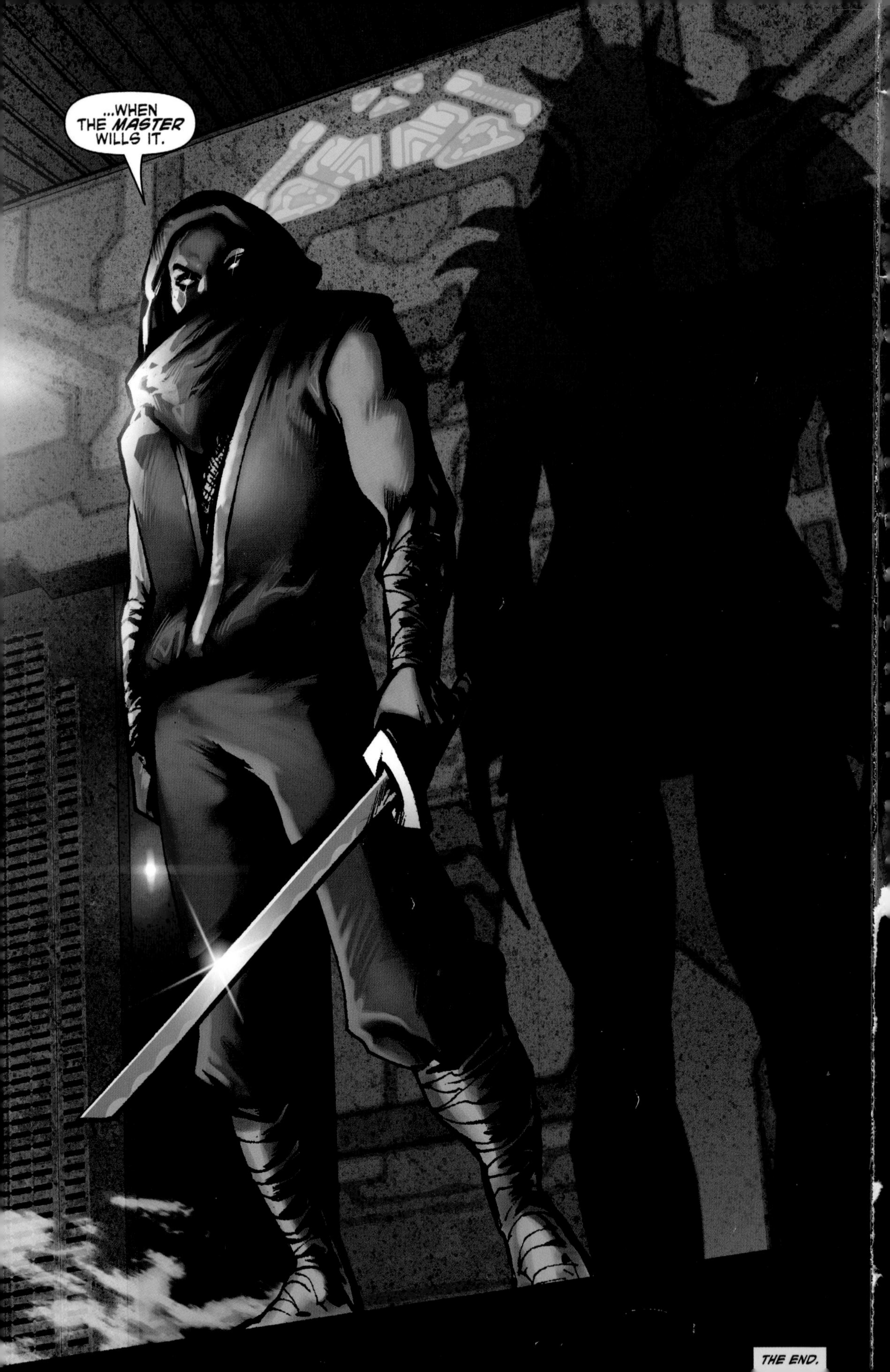
...WHEN THE MASTER WILLS IT.
THE END.

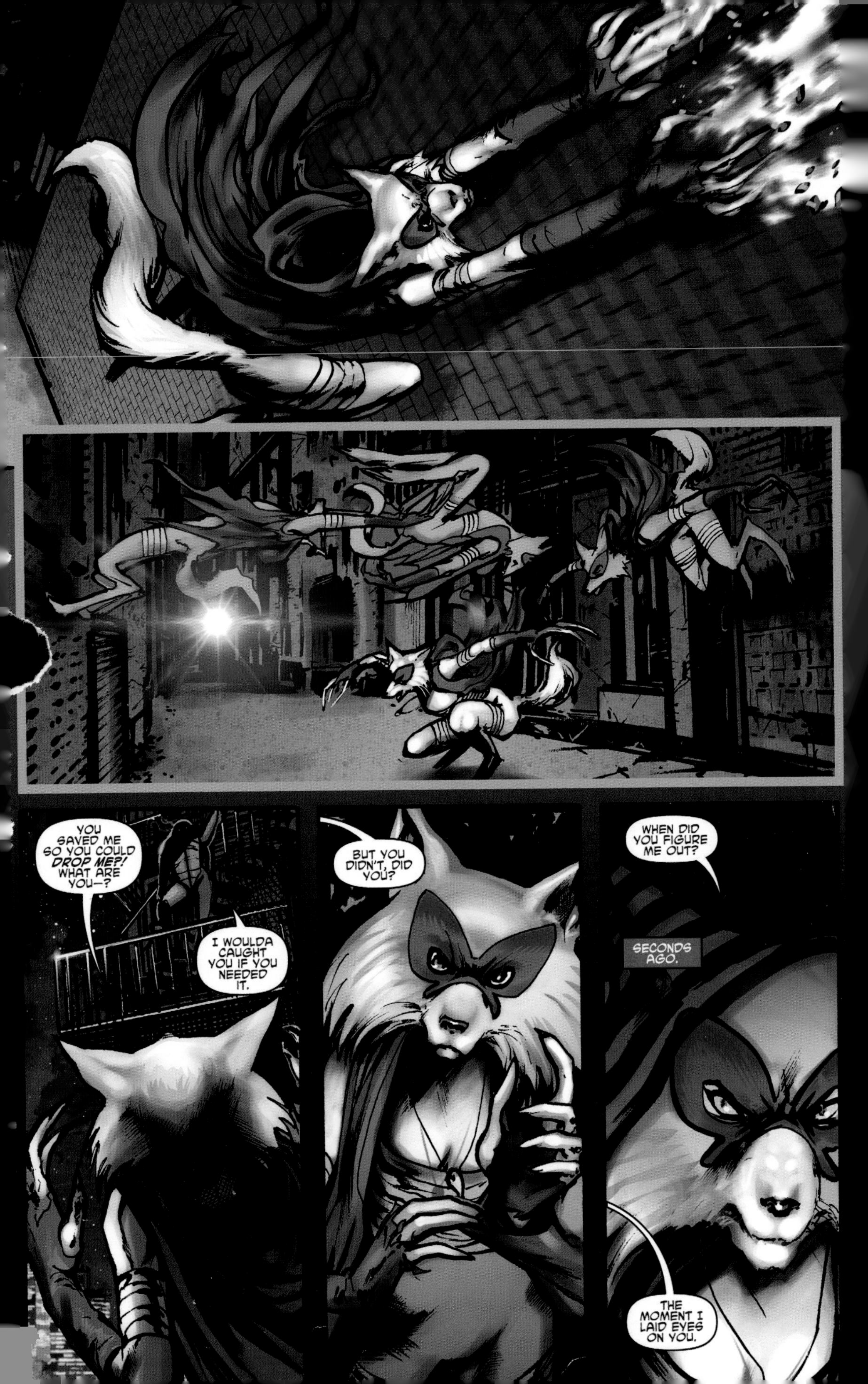

YOU SAVED ME SO YOU COULD DROP ME?! WHAT ARE YOU--?
I WOULDA CAUGHT YOU IF YOU NEEDED IT.
BUT YOU DIDN'T, DID YOU?
WHEN DID YOU FIGURE ME OUT?
SECONDS AGO.
THE MOMENT I LAID EYES ON YOU.

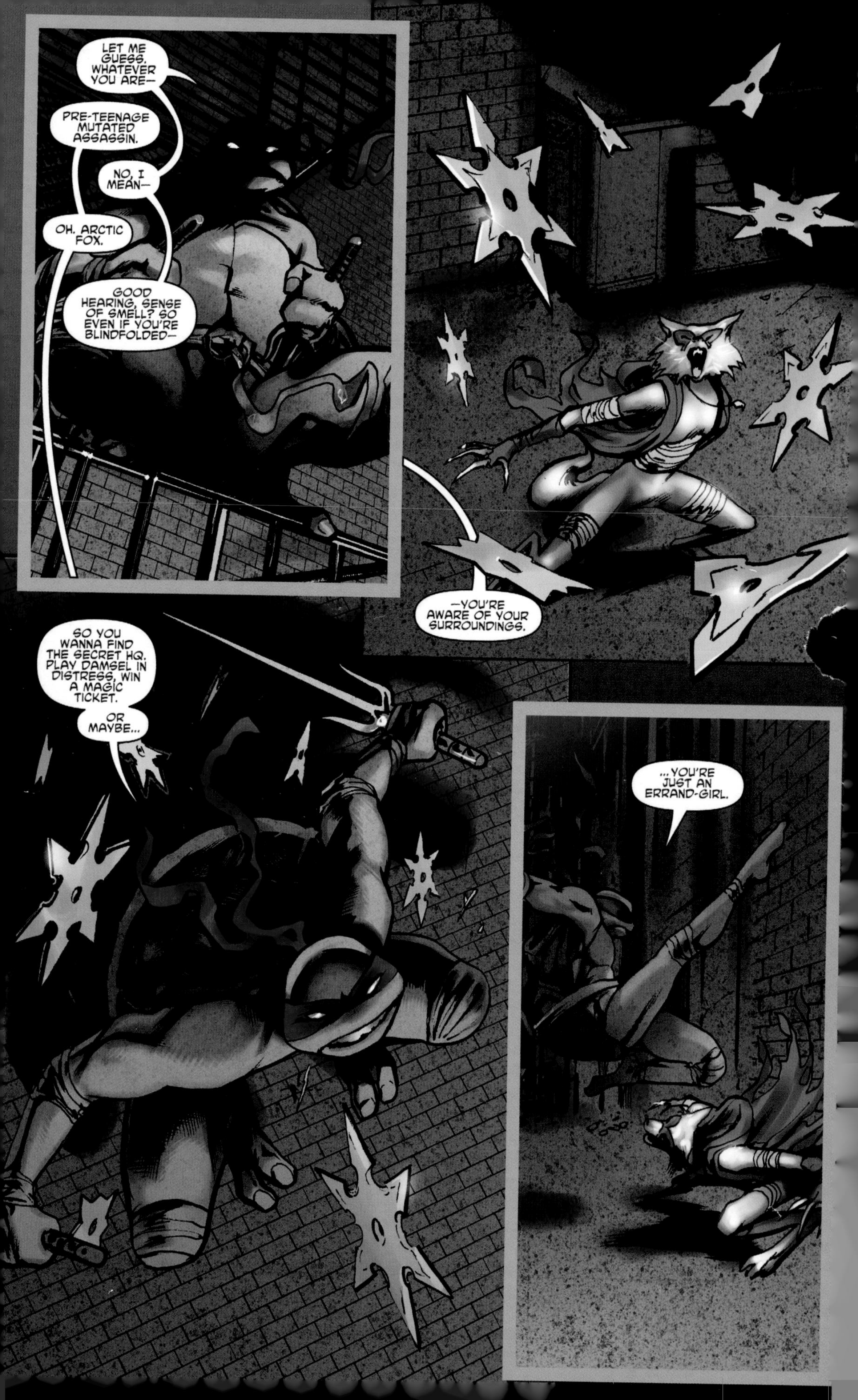
LET ME GUESS. WHATEVER YOU ARE—
PRE-TEENAGE MUTATED ASSASSIN.
NO, I MEAN—
OH. ARCTIC FOX.
GOOD HEARING, SENSE OF SMELL? SO EVEN IF YOU'RE BLINDFOLDED—
—YOU'RE AWARE OF YOUR SURROUNDINGS.
SO YOU WANNA FIND THE SECRET HQ. PLAY DAMSEL IN DISTRESS, WIN A MAGIC TICKET.
OR MAYBE...
...YOU'RE JUST AN ERRAND-GIRL.

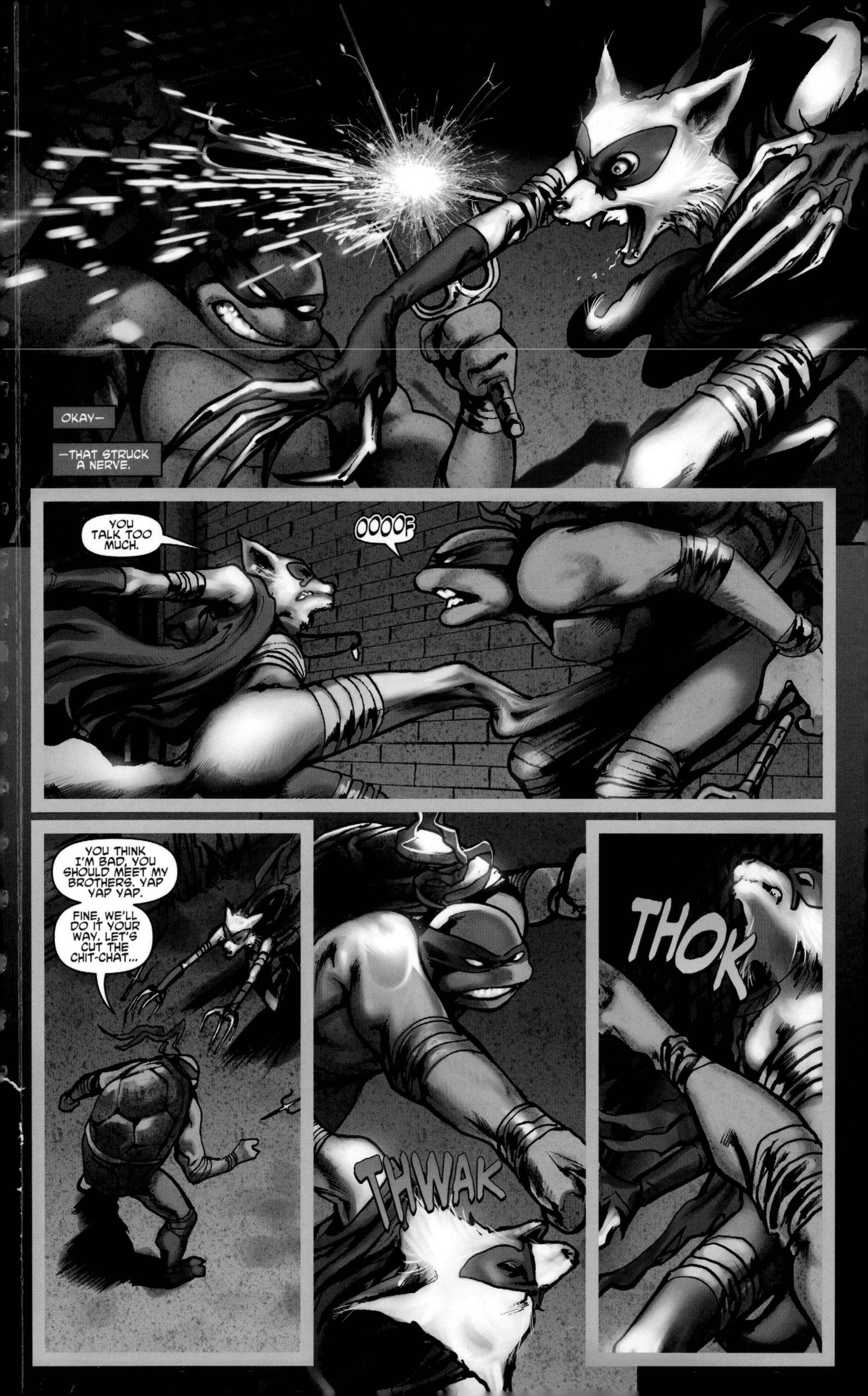
OKAY—
—THAT STRUCK A NERVE.
YOU TALK TOO MUCH.
OOOOF
YOU THINK I'M BAD, YOU SHOULD MEET MY BROTHERS. YAP YAP YAP.
FINE, WE'LL DO IT YOUR WAY. LET'S CUT THE CHIT-CHAT...
THWAK
THOK

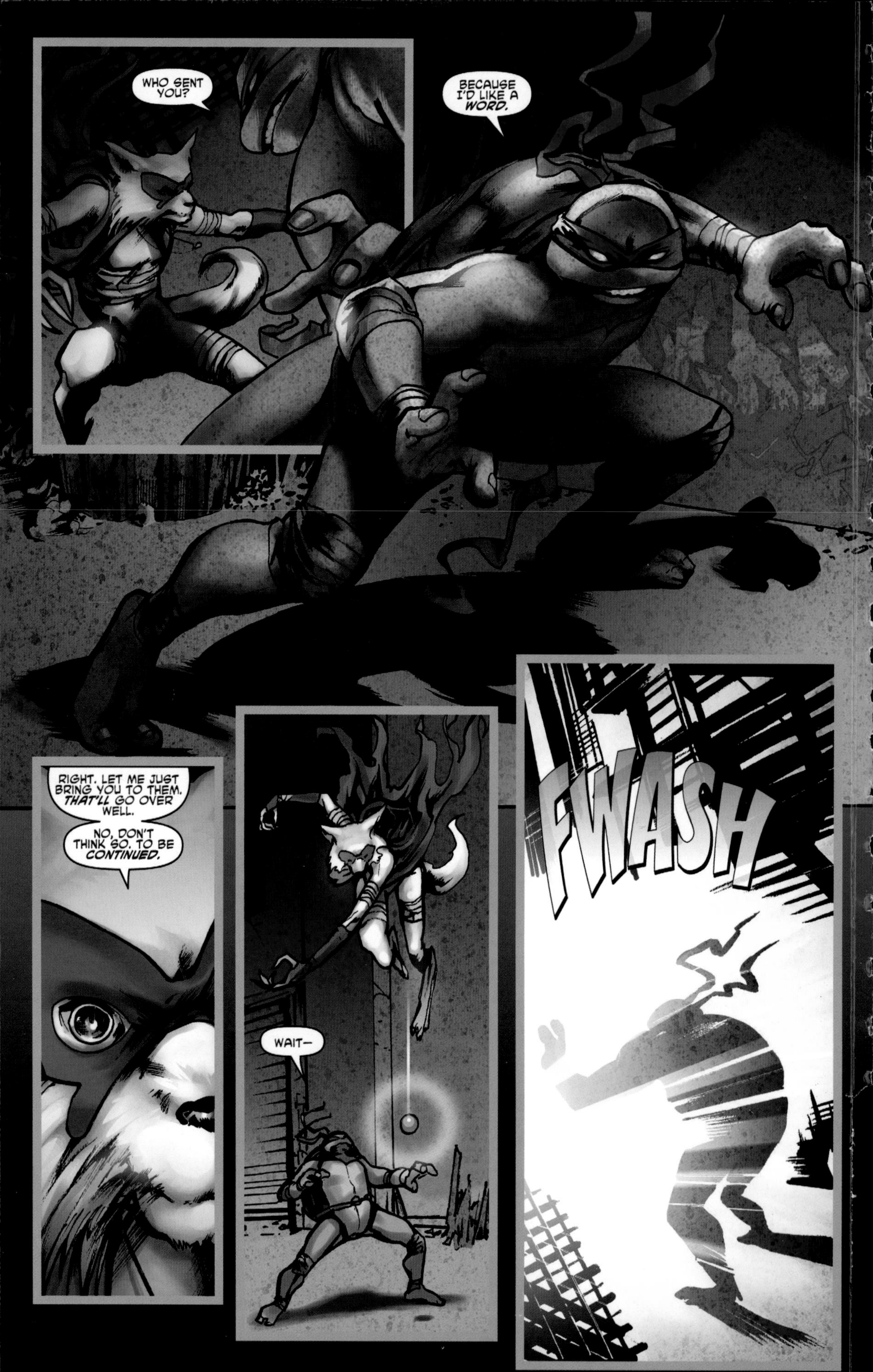
WHO SENT YOU?
BECAUSE I'D LIKE A *WORD.*
RIGHT. LET ME JUST BRING YOU TO THEM. *THAT'LL* GO OVER WELL.
NO, DON'T THINK SO. TO BE *CONTINUED.*
WAIT–
FWASH

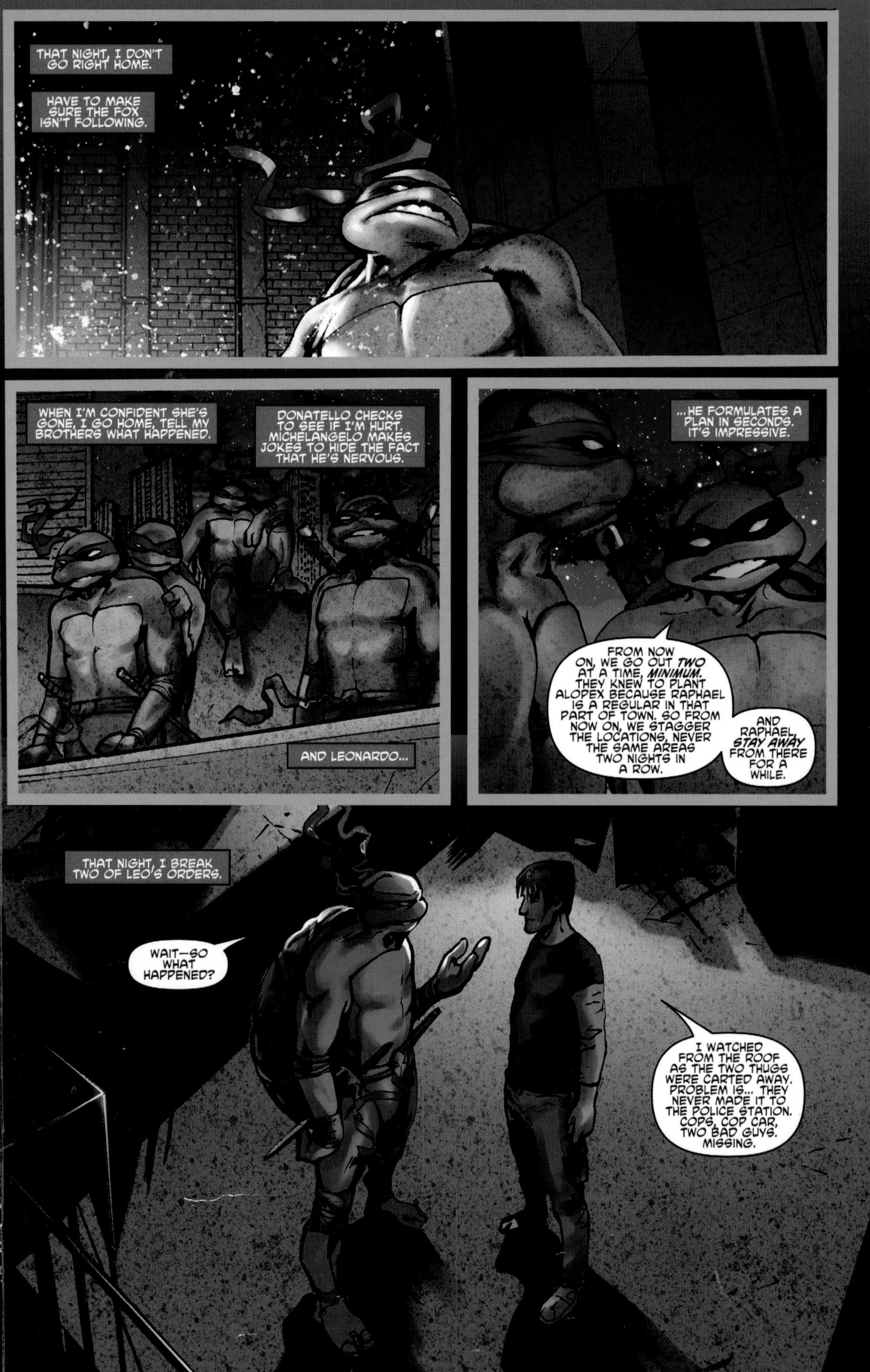
THAT NIGHT, I DON'T GO RIGHT HOME.
HAVE TO MAKE SURE THE FOX ISN'T FOLLOWING.
WHEN I'M CONFIDENT SHE'S GONE, I GO HOME, TELL MY BROTHERS WHAT HAPPENED.
DONATELLO CHECKS TO SEE IF I'M HURT. MICHELANGELO MAKES JOKES TO HIDE THE FACT THAT HE'S NERVOUS.
AND LEONARDO...
...HE FORMULATES A PLAN IN SECONDS. IT'S IMPRESSIVE.
FROM NOW ON, WE GO OUT TWO AT A TIME, MINIMUM. THEY KNEW TO PLANT ALOPEX BECAUSE RAPHAEL IS A REGULAR IN THAT PART OF TOWN. SO FROM NOW ON, WE STAGGER THE LOCATIONS, NEVER THE SAME AREAS TWO NIGHTS IN A ROW.
AND RAPHAEL, STAY AWAY FROM THERE FOR A WHILE.
THAT NIGHT, I BREAK TWO OF LEO'S ORDERS.
WAIT—SO WHAT HAPPENED?
I WATCHED FROM THE ROOF AS THE TWO THUGS WERE CARTED AWAY. PROBLEM IS... THEY NEVER MADE IT TO THE POLICE STATION. COPS, COP CAR, TWO BAD GUYS. MISSING.

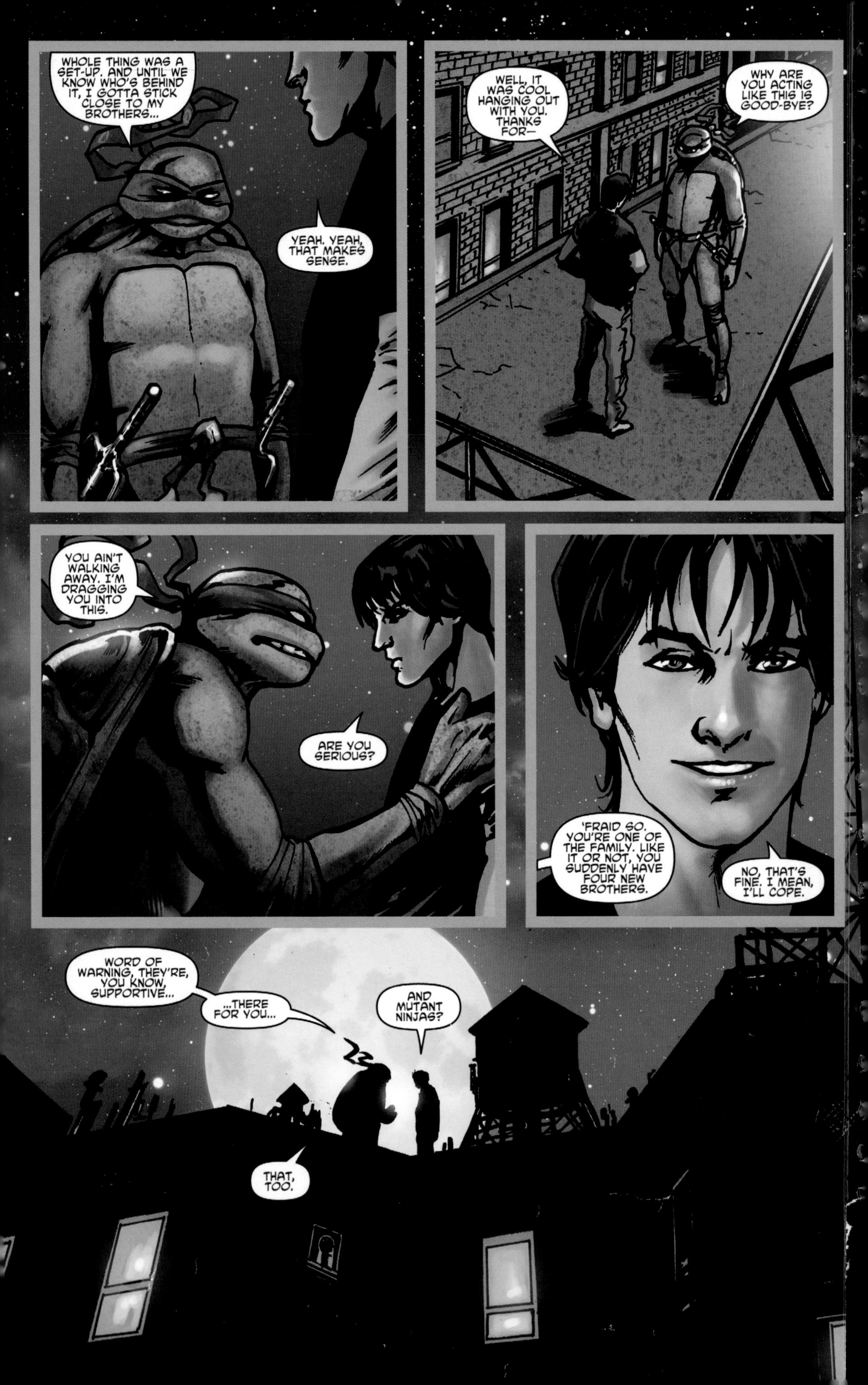
WHOLE THING WAS A SET-UP. AND UNTIL WE KNOW WHO'S BEHIND IT, I GOTTA STICK CLOSE TO MY BROTHERS...
YEAH. YEAH, THAT MAKES SENSE.
WELL, IT WAS COOL HANGING OUT WITH YOU. THANKS FOR—
WHY ARE YOU ACTING LIKE THIS IS GOOD-BYE?
YOU AIN'T WALKING AWAY. I'M DRAGGING YOU INTO THIS.
ARE YOU SERIOUS?
'FRAID SO. YOU'RE ONE OF THE FAMILY. LIKE IT OR NOT, YOU SUDDENLY HAVE FOUR NEW BROTHERS.
NO, THAT'S FINE. I MEAN, I'LL COPE.
WORD OF WARNING, THEY'RE, YOU KNOW, SUPPORTIVE...
...THERE FOR YOU...
AND MUTANT NINJAS?
THAT, TOO.